Gypsy Mercer

Surviving the Storm

Musings of a Gypsy Soul

By Gypsy Mercer

Gypsy Mercer

Surviving the Storm/Gypsy Mercer ~ First Edition
ISBN: 978-1072542360

Dedication

To the beautiful, brilliant and amazing people who will forever reside in my heart and soul

To the ones who stole my heart, sometimes leaving lessons in their wake, some leaving the most vivid memories to re-live at my leisure

I thank you all ♥ ♥ ♥

With love, Always

~ Gypsy

Gypsy Mercer

<u>Other books by Gypsy Mercer</u>

Into the Fire: Musings of a Gypsy Soul (2018)

Foreward

If you are a fan of Gypsy Mercer's writing, you'll be in for a treat with her new collection, *Surviving the Storm*. Make yourself comfortable, pour yourself a cup of coffee or sip on your favorite tea, then bask in these endearing thoughts from the heart by Gypsy Mercer. Gypsy opens each chapter with a different storm, and from there, it's a whirlwind of love, loss, survival and strength. She even adds a touch of playfulness with some flirty, sensual, lusty poems. I particularly liked the poem, 'Are you Real'. In this poem, Gypsy poses the question, 'was this love real or just a fabrication of the imagination'. In 'Come Closer' and 'Jealousy, she exposed her vulnerability, for what is poetry without a hint of madness and a sense of raw vulnerability?

Gypsy's poetry seems to be a reminder that we all get sucked into our own inner battles, like a tornado, hurricane, or tsunami. Sometimes we are ripped apart by love itself; that no one is immune from struggle and heartbreak. I hear the voice of a woman who has gone to war with herself, who has been betrayed by love, and through her own turmoil, soul searching and self-reflection, has ultimately found the courage, wisdom and compassion that has made her the beautiful "storm" she is. Her experiences are human; they are relatable and easily enjoyable to read.

Gypsy's 'Lone Wolf Series' and 'Just Because' chapters at the end of the book were like the clearing after a storm. It was a nice way to synchronize and end this precious collection of thoughts.

Gypsy is the calm before the storm, the center of the storm, and the storm itself. She is a woman who has gone to war with her heart and conquered the demons of being broken by love, yet still hopeful that love will once again find its way to her heart. I hope you enjoy Gypsy's second poetry collection, *Surviving the Storm* as much as I did.

Melody Lee, author of *Season of the Sorceress, Vine: Book of Poetry, and Moon Gypsy.*

<u>SECTIONS</u>

Gypsy Mercer

Hurricanes

The hurricane is the most violent of tropical cyclones. It is also known as a typhoon in the South Pacific, and as a willy-willy in Australia. High winds, heavy rainfall and ocean swells herald the fury, destruction and death unleashed during these storms. Until 40+ years ago, hurricanes were always named after women.

11

Gypsy Mercer

HESITATION

She hesitates to open the door
She knows what lies beyond it
She knows she has a choice
But is she brave enough
   Strong enough
To live with her decision
A lifetime of love
   Or an eternity of lies
She hesitates
And shuts the door

PRICE OF YOUR SOUL

You think we are alike?

You only know my public side

Smiling

Poised

But that is just the wrapping

My layers run deep

Each one requires a special permission

A sacred key or handshake

Sometimes my blood boils

Sometimes my icicles pierce

Your tenderest skin

The smile and poise are lies

Masks

Empty promises

Designed as road blocks

Or as the sweetest dessert

You need me to want you

More than you need yourself

What are you willing to wager
To take the next step?
What is the price of your soul?
What can you live without?
What can you live with?
Decide before you unleash my beast

<u>CAUTERIZE</u>

Loving you was my gift to myself

Your smile lifted my spirit

Your kiss warmed my heart

Your spirit gave me strength

Your energy empowered me

Your eyes were my pathway into believing

But your lies pierced my heart

Your body smelled of her perfume

Your words were programmed and

Rehearsed

You left me behind

You forgot me

Now I must cauterize myself

From feeling

Until this madness

This sadness

Vacates my soul

SACHET

I locked you away
With sachet and handkerchiefs
And school girl dreams
I guarded the box fiercely
From my heart and thoughts
Until the day
When I felt alone
Unloved
Undervalued
I opened the box
And
You emerged
Full grown
And
Just as dangerous

ICE PRINCESS

The world is not large enough for you and
me
We are so powerful
    In our love
    In our hate
We love without bounds
We hate without remorse
    Our love builds bridges
    Our hate builds armor
Both destructive without reins
Both fed by the same intensity
Both fueled by the same fire

Lowering the bridge to admit you
    The gentleness, the rage
Both part of love
    And the curse of love
Love is both the answer
    And the defeat

Erect my castle made of steel and tears
The Ice Maiden is in residence
Awaiting
The arrival of her triumphant King

<u>DON'T MAKE ME CHOOSE</u>

Sometimes I write
To purge you from my system
Other times I refuse
To write
So you cannot hijack
My thoughts
My heart
Oft times
I cast you in my dreams

Today I am conflicted
Just knowing you exist
In full metal jacket
Deep in my soul

<u>I DID NOT RUN</u>

I know you for what you are
And I'm still here
I did not run for shelter
I took you as you are
I am not fooled by your demeanor
I know the strength and power
You wield in the your world
Outside ours
And I know my heart lies safe
Within yours

<u>HURRICANE DAY</u>

I want it hard

Fast

Total surrender

Forgetting my name

Lost to our surroundings

Your animal unleashing my animal

Blood surging through our veins

Moans

Screams

Crying your name

Nails marking your back

Muscles burning

Momentum rising

Release

Crashing

Surrender

PATTERNS

Please don't feel so deeply
I know your pain
And it breaks my heart
All along I tried to shelter you
Hoping you would recognize my distance
I was not trying to play hard to get
There was no getting to be got
I loved the good man in you
After years of bad boys
But it is hard to break a pattern
It is difficult to accept pliancy
When it is fire that feeds my soul
It was hard to understand constraints
When I love to kiss the edge
Please go
Don't look back
Find your princess
I need no knight
To slay my dragons

<u>CONNECTION</u>

Our connection is intense
Yet as subtle as a siren's call
It is knowing
    More than feeling
It is in the silence
    Not the knowing
It is the sensation
    Behind the feeling
It is the peace
    The completeness
    The rightness
That infuses my thoughts
    At the mere whisper
    Of your presence
    And your touch

MY CONFESSION

My confession
You are my obsession
Lighting my life
Creating strife

Magically close
Immeasurably distant
Stealing my thoughts
Capturing my heart

A prison so beautifully created
Awaited
But a prison nonetheless

UNPREPARED

Holding on tightly

Not letting anyone in

Takes a strength

Hercules did not possess

Walls are manmade

And therefore flawed

Cracks appear

Erosion weakens the foundation

And one day

A gentle push

Collapses all your defenses

Leaving you naked

Unarmed

Unprepared

For the flood of emotions

That you held captive
For so long
Escaping
And you break
And you cry
And you let someone in

<u>JOURNEY</u>

Leave me alone

This journey is a solitary one

It will be the hardest and longest walk

I have ever taken

I must be strong

Strong enough to avoid temptation

Strong enough to continue on

After my heart has been ruptured

My illusions obliterated

My trust demolished

But continue I must

You see I must make sense of it all

Must determine where to place

The shattered pieces

Be it Broken Dreams?

Or Lofty Promises?

Or Innocence Stolen?

Or the Devil's due?

I will clean up this mess

You only complicate things

You always have

Because I wanted to believe in you

    Trust you

    Love you

    Live my life with you

My journey is of self discovery

Am I as bright as I think I am?

As strong?

As ruthless?

As independent?

Tomorrow is another day

I will know more then

<u>MY KIND OF MAGIC</u>

Loving you is my kind of magic
Feeling your presence
  without your touch
Hearing your voice
  without your words
Inhaling your fragrance
    on last night's sheets
Feeling your touch
   without your presence
Hearing your words
   without your voice
Knowing your love
   scattered throughout
The sands of time

FEVERISH

Hidden beneath the covers

Is my man

Feverish to my delight

Playful as is his nature

Hide and seek is his game

Teasing me

Luring me in

Locking the door

Letting the fun begin

UNFOLDING

There is as much beauty as

There is pain

In his unfolding

Feeling the depths of despair

The deceit

The destruction

The cruelty

Though he does not forgive

Nor does he forget

Or confuse the intent

His story holds so much love

For it is impossible

To hurt so much

If not for a tender heart

And pure soul

His joy over a smile or laugh

His skin tingling with the touch

And feel of brisk air

Fused with damp snow

On a star lit night

And the gentle tease of fur

Against your skin

The warmest breath on your neck

The wettest, softest kiss

To heal you

Or make amends

And

Bring you peace

That is what my heart wants

And needs

TEARDROPS

I reach out to touch you
    But you have gone
You did not wait for the storm to pass
Leaving teardrop upon the glass

You expected perfection
    Something I could not offer
For my heart gets messy
    In the throes of sacred love

You did not wait
For the euphoria to settle
Assuming the worst
You made your escape

You erected a wall
    Too steep for me to traverse
Letting me know
    I meant nothing to you at all

KINGS AND QUEENS

We emerge

As Kings and Queens

When our egos are released

Our minds are open

Our hearts are ready

To unite

To merge

To sync

Our spirit

And live

As one being

Flowing greedily

<u>ARE YOU REAL</u>

Do you even exist
  In a real flesh and blood world
Did we really meet
     Laugh

     Make love

     Fall in love

     Make promises

     Get lost chasing rainbows
Did we really wake on the beach
  Waves crashing on our bodies
Did we really hike to the top of the mountain
  Make love leaning against a tree
Did we ever steam the windows
  In the backseat of a car
Were we ever so hungry for each other
  That food was forgotten
Did we ever kiss in public
  And forget that we were

Did we tease truckers on highways
    With our antics
Did we giggle, kiss, cry, and caress
Are you real
    Or my imagination
You must be real because I
    Still remember
    Still taste you
    Still feel you
    Still want you
My imagination is simply not that vivid

<u>I BELIEVE IN YOU</u>

I believe in you

To love

And protect me

I trust you

Enough

To walk at your side

And follow your lead

I honor you

By accepting you

As my true mate

And fighting

And living

And loving

As one

<u>HOBBY</u>

You were his hobby
Not his wife
Not his life
He could put you on a shelf
When he was tired of playing
Real life versus fantasy
Dreams versus reality
But a man has to eat

<u>COME HOME</u>

I ache for you

Please come home

Because I am your home

Leaving room for no other

In my heart

Because I am filled

With your need

Your heart

My soul

My fire

<u>DISGUISE</u>

If I am your addiction

Then why do I crave

Your love

Cruising through my veins

Filling my heart

And soul

With love

With lies

Why are we not comfortable

With truth

Bold and bare

Trusting

One another

To love each other

As we truly are

Without the veil

Without the disguise

<u>TONIGHT</u>

We have tonight

To get it right

Love is not strong enough to save us

But it is the glue that will bind us

Let it be the bond that fills us

    With trust

    With respect

    With passion

    With understanding

Let it not fall prey

    To jealousy

    To deceit

    To anger

    To lies

Tonight let us commit

To love, honor and cherish

From this day forward

Until the end of time

DREAMER

If I am a dreamer
    Then you are my muse
With eyes wide open
    I embrace you
You color my sunsets
In hues so passionate
    That lover's cry
    In expectation and hope
In silent prayer
    I beacon you to my side
Touching me with your
    Strength and wisdom
You allow me to glide
Knowing you are the
    Breath that lifts me
    The kiss that breaks my fall
Your heart
    Encompassing my soul

<u>SOULMATE</u>

My soulmate
So far away
Yet ever so close
Sharing dreams
   And ideas
Needing only half
   As the other completes
Feeling moods
Understanding needs
Knowing how to offer
   What is needed
   Knowing when
Safety and openness
   Lacking fear or censor
Just understanding
   And acceptance
Share my world now
Complete the circle

<u>COME CLOSER</u>

Come closer
        But not too close
                I run when I am scared
Talk with me
        But don't expect to hear my secrets
Walk with me
        But not too close
                I need my space
Listen to me
        But don't dwell on my silences
Touch me
        But be gentle yet sure
Love me
        But don't expect love
                Until I feel it
Run away with me
        But keep up
                For we will soar
                        Beyond our imagination

45

<u>WISER</u>

The sadder but wiser man
Will be the one to capture my heart
He has known pain and heartache
Yet chooses to love again
He will be tentative
At first
Growing bolder
With each kiss
Until he is sure
That I am sure
Then he will turn the tables
And take command
Of my heart
And soul

GYPSY NIGHTS

Gypsy nights
Promised delights
Teasing kisses
Near misses
Desires build fires
Lips divine like expensive wine
Bad behavior is my savior

Too old to play
    Patty cake games
I want the fire
    I want the fight
Let it be just us tonight
And share morning light

Gypsy Mercer

<u>SECOND CHANCES</u>

So many years ago

We parted

Different goals

Changing values

But the love never died

Nor did it grow dormant

It lies in the recesses of my heart

Drowning in my tears

Compromising my happiness

Hope is its best friend

Knowing

The moon would cycle

The tides would erode my pain

The sun would rise once more

Knowing

We were not over

And would open the door to

Second chances

ADDICT

It seems my hands are on automatic

Needing to feel you

Needing to touch you

Stroking your arm

Following the lines on your palm

Fingers through your hair

Outlining your lips

And like an addict

Kissing you so deeply

That I lose

My breath

My sanity

In a schism of time

PENETRATION

Not mired in emotion
Nor remembrance
Rather soul deep penetration
Into my core
Flowing into my veins
Traveling to my heart and limbs
Leaving me paralyzed
Capturing me unaware
And ready

SCARED

Dare I hope

Dare I pray

This time will be different

A new Chapter

Or

A finished story

Just talk

You say

Do you remember when

What did you mean by what

Why didn't we fight for us

Will the answers change anything

Will we be able to forgive

Now that we understand

Can we forget

Are you ready

Because I am scared

<u>YOUR SECRET</u>

I am ever as powerful as you

Lest you forget

It was me

Who brought you to your knees

Nursing your wounds

Putting your needs first

Encouraging

Molding

Feeding

Loving

You healed

You grew stronger

You put yourself first

Always returning at night

You always had a thirst

To feed on my elixir

Leaving at dawn

Battle gear on

No one the wiser

The source of your strength

Your secret well

Carefully hidden

Lest others learn

Your secret

Your obsession

My power

<u>JEALOUS</u>

She may satisfy your body
Be the one you reach for
    to comfort you during the night
But it is me that answers your souls call
Does she know I am in your heart
And your head
Does she know you race time to share
    Your thoughts
    Your ideas
    Your feelings
        With me?
Tell me why she should be able feel
    Your touch
    Your kiss
Yet I experience your deepest passion
That thrills long after your body is sated
Why are you able to converse with her
    On multiple subjects with British
 precision

Yet our conversations are without structure
They traverse between child-like wonder
    and galactic knowledge
Riddled with laughter and respect
I have the best of you
Freely given
Without end
Tell me luv, why am I still jealous of her?

Gypsy Mercer

<u>MISTAKES</u>

This time

We will make it work

Not because we do everything

    Perfectly

But rather because

We want this

    More

Than our missteps

    Before

We did not make

A lot of mistakes

But the ones we did make

Were monumental

They are behind us

Our mistakes will be new

Will be well thought out

Will be well placed

To cause the least ripple

Because we want this

Because we need this

We will accept nothing less

This time

Gypsy Mercer

Tornadoes

Tornadoes are extremely dangerous, with winds that often exceed 300 mph, the ominous funnel leaving destruction and chaos in its wake.

Gypsy Mercer

HUNGER

I have a hunger

Gnawing at my soul

A primal need

An emptiness so deep

That only you can fill

Long ago

We were one

But the universe had other plans

Our love fractured

Yet our souls remained entwined

Awaiting another day

Let it be today

I am tired of living a half life

Filled with sadness

And longing

Touch me again

And make it last

<u>DARK EYES</u>

Your eyes are so dark

They are nearly black

They speak to me

Of passion

Of fury

Of pain

And I cannot resist...

I melt and absorb your every emotion

Knowing I lose me

In the process

Sharing your feelings

Stroking your anger

Lost in your passion

Drowning in the abyss

<u>LAVA</u>

The depth of my love
      And
The intensity of my love
      For you
Scares me so
And when I feel
The depth and intensity
Of your love
I shake with fear
That our love for each other
This uncontrolled fire
This hunger for unification
This soul merge
This free flowing lava
Will cause us to implode
Destroying our love
Slaying us in the process

<u>NOT THAT KIND OF WOMAN</u>

I'm not the kind of woman you can own
I'm either romanced
Or consumed
Oft times both
I play when it suits me
And the player is skilled
    Confident
    Uninhibited
You are not strong enough to hold
    My heart
    My attention
    My interest
    My time
You may have the power
To bring me to my knees
But I am a Phoenix
I will rise
And torch your soul
Searing my memory in your heart
Tainting all that follow

FOG

The sun had set

The rain heaved its last tear

The crickets and frogs yet to appear

The only sounds were in my head

The ones I wanted to forget

I wrestled with the memories

Twisting and turning

But never changing

Words I could not forget

Words I'd come to regret

Looking outside my tortured soul

Fog rolling in

Settling near the ground

My heart a wasteland

Wishing the fog to come

Lay it to rest

And heave its last tear

I CHEATED

I am so sad
Because I know
You are with someone else
I know it was never
Possible
Between us
But that didn't stop
My imagination
Or cool my dreams
The perfect friendship
The loyal confident
Yet I cheated
And gave you a part of my heart
You never asked for
Or wanted
And loving you
Was not an option
Just my reality
As my tears fall
Silently

THE SIN

You are the man I wanted
But I was scared and ran
You never understood
That I needed
You to show me
You would never let me go
But we were young
We didn't understand
Our romantic hearts
Or the sin
Our innocence would birth
You thought I meant to go
I just needed you to make me
Want to stay

<u>DOORS</u>

I need to only know
What he is to me
Don't try to dilute
My happiness
With your
Tales and tattletales
Everyone deserves to be
Reborn in every relationship
First kiss
First surrender
First tear
I always open my own doors

<u>SHIELDS</u>

Close that door

Throw away all the keys

Let there be just you and me

Laughing

Crying

Loving

Without the shields

We left on the other side

<u>CHOOSE</u>

Choose to love me
> Or
Choose to leave me
No more inconsistencies
As I interpret your intentions
While you ride the fence
Spilling half-baked promises
Watching me drown
> All in
>> Or
> All out
>>> Leave me whole
>>> Or
>>> Leave me alone

<u>THE MOON</u>

The moon

In her wisdom

Creates hopes and dreams

And

Should darkness fall

She sends the moon back to us

Brighter and more intense

To illuminate our path

With faith

Reminding us to be strong

MANMADE WALLS

Holding on tightly

Not letting anyone in

Takes a strength Hercules did not possess

Walls are manmade

And therefore flawed

Cracks appear

Erosion weakens the foundation

And one day

A gentle push

Collapses all your defenses

Leaving you naked

And unarmed

Unprepared

For the flood of emotions

Escaping that you held captive

For so long

And you break

And you cry

And you let someone in

TRUTH or LIES

Truth

Shrouded in words

Meant to distort

Deceive

Tease

Please

Lies

Spoken so sweetly

So earnestly

So expertly

So twisted

So naturally

In the end

You choose

What you need

To believe

SNARE

You kissed me and I knew it was a mistake
But your Bad Boy taste was delicious
And tasted like more
You captured my imagination
And my body followed
As did my treacherous heart
Trapped in your snare
I had nowhere else
I wanted to be

CHANGE

The mundane
That is what I cannot handle
I need change
Choice
I need ignition
Else I slowly die a life mired in Mediocrity
I need to experience those things
That light up my soul
I need to know that
Tomorrow will be different
Yet the same in the good things
I need progress
Metamorphosis
Transformation
I want peace and tranquility
Where there are no surprises
I need to understand
Those things that happen in my life
Make sense of my chaos
And I need you
Like the air I breathe

<u>**OVERDRAWN**</u>

To have and to hold
'Til death do us part
And part we did
Said goodbye to tomorrow
Letting yesterday remain in my past
My love died of deceit
Promises made and broken
And the destruction you lobbed
Into our life
Healing and forgetting
Are my goals
Just not for you
Our account is overdrawn

MY PRAYER

When the tide rolled in

You were nothing more than a dream

Albeit a nightly dream

An escape

My prayer

Where my happiness lies

Awaiting

Nightfall

<u>MAKE BELIEVE</u>

We are make believe
We are fantasy
We are not meant to be

I listen to your words with my heart
I listen to your thoughts
    as they reach your eyes
I listen to your moans as we make love

I feel your touch
I sense your urgency
I cry your name
This is insane

QUIET

You are probably right about a great deal of quiet settling on us. This particular holiday season feels differently than the rest. I feel answers are in the air waiting for us to recognize them. I believe your words, along with other wordsmith's, allow us to live in an alternate reality where there is no judgement, only feelings. We go beyond our body to the garden within our mind. When we have had our fill, we return and reward ourselves with the feel of flesh and the scent of desire.

<u>TIMING</u>

Feeling the connection
From so far away
Knowing you feel it too
Timing is not on our side
Once we had a moment
And forfeited it
But the connection never broke
    Living lives
    Living lies
And the years went by
    Near misses
    Aborted searches
Time turned the page
And we finally found each other
    Fear stepped in
    Once again
Is our timing finally right
Or will fate spite?

FAIR TRADE

If I give you everything
Your heart desires
Then I become your heart's desire
Seems a fair trade
Your soul for my heart

Gypsy Mercer

THE MAN

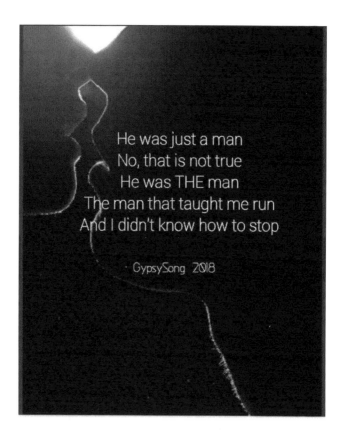

He was just a man
No, that is not true
He was THE man
The man that taught me run
And I didn't know how to stop

GypsySong 2018

ANSWERS

I have always felt incomplete

Missing the critical puzzle piece

That translates confusion

From madness to clarity

The piece that makes me whole

Answering questions

I did not know to ask

Or feared to ask

The diamond in my elusive armor

Just beyond my reach

The image behind the blur

The gasp before my sigh

STRANDED

Stranded on a life raft alone

Watching the waves

Peak and break

My salty tears

My sunburned face

Remembering that

    I tried

    I tried to save you

    I tried to save us

But wishes don't always

Come true

Some simply are pulled

Back into the ocean

    Restructured

    Relaunched

Into something new

Something whole

<u>FREE WILL</u>

I'll tell you true
I'm scared of you
You reached out
My heart beat faster
Hoping against hope
To right a wrong
I had no free will
I had to answer
I could not have
Choreographed
A more perfect conversation
I gave you the answers
I had withheld
Plans made
Days faded
Now I am captive
To your free will
  Waiting

<u>EROSION</u>

She left because his demons were

Gnawing away at her core

Slowly like erosion

She knew because each day she woke

Battle worn and sad

Until the sadness became her reality

A new life

New scenery

The occasional lover

Never lessened her guilt

The guilt she wore because

She wasn't strong enough

To stay at his side

The love never died or diminished

When finally he arose as Victor

He bid her hello

And new possibilities formed

Sometimes time is the answer

CLOAK

Through this door

Are my hopes

Dreams

Fears

Insecurities

I leave behind

Disappointment

And sorrow

That cloaked me

Weighing me down

Crushing me

I will take the lessons

The experiences

And craft a world

Of love

And respect

From the crumbling walls

That nearly destroyed me

<u>BURIAL</u>

Don't forget your dreams
    For another
They will remain deep inside
    Festering and growing
Until the day
    You implode
    Or explode
And face the reality
    The price of this burial
Sift through the remains/ashes
And decide again
Which truly soothes
Your soul

SINGLE THREAD

Hanging on by a single thread
Surviving life's battles
Still wanting to go on
Hell bent on beating the odds
Tying a knot for good measure
Not losing my spot
Not losing my focus
No slips or falls
Continuing my climb
Giving my all
Grabbing the brass ring
Breaking my fall

COLORS

Colors fade with time
Memories fade as well
But they malinger
And are as ever present
   As the tides
Sometimes bright
Bold
Passionate
Painful
Then they ebb
And we are lulled
   Into complacency
Thinking we are now free
Believing they have now died
Hoping they live on
   In someone else's dreams
Where we colored the outcome
   Differently
Through salty tears and longing

HONOR

He is a man devoid of honor

A crime against God

A crime against nature

Hidden behind laughter

Ever the raconteur

Truth but a fiction

His weapons deceit and stealth

As he lures you into his black web of lies

Taking his pleasure

Taking his prize

Winning is his game

Then he met Her

But it was too late

The dye he set

Did not allow for fate

Gypsy Mercer

Thunderstorms

Thunderstorms incite different types of weather, although thunder and lightning are often present, they are usually accompanied by strong winds, heavy rain, including snow, sleet and hail.

93

Gypsy Mercer

THE STORM

Waiting for the skies to clear

Granting me reprieve

From restless thoughts

Hastening my calm

Subduing my memories

Offering me peace

Until the next storm threatens

Erasing it all

Gypsy Mercer

APPLE IN EDEN

Glistening lips hovering over mine

Beckoning like the apple in Eden

Rapturous by design

Poisonous to the core

The death of innocence

<u>FORTUNETELLER</u>

She sees you coming
She hears your secrets
Holding your hand
Looking into your eyes
Weaving her magic
Making demands
She promises you dreams
But won't say when
Just to trust the journey
And see where it ends

<u>STORMS RAGE</u>

Colorless stories
Colorful emotions
Drinking love's potion
Reliving past glories

                    Storms rage
                    Brilliant skies
                    Cruel lies
              Time to turn the page

I ran out of time
I ran out of rhyme
Hoping our story ended differently
With less duplicity

SPLINTERS

Why did you open the door
When you never meant to stay
    You pounded
    You insisted
    You persisted
Leaving splinters in your wake
    A mess
        And heartbreak

THE MIST

I sense the rain coming to an end
The feeling of control is returning
Maybe it is time for a new chapter
Maybe not
My soul raged a fierce battle
Trying to protect my heart
Logic battled with serendipity
To make sense of yesterday
Hoping to file it as complete

But the mist is still in the air
Keeping my heart pliant
And soul tender
Dreaming of tomorrows

FREEZING

It's cold outside
My heart is freezing
Please let me in
Your warmth and fire
Will melt this ice
Igniting my flame
Once again

<u>RAINDROPS</u>

Warm and gentle was the rain
Soothing, wet
Inviting dreams of us
In youthful embrace

Winds increased
Chills crept in
Raindrops like cannons on a tin roof
Heart raced
Remembering our last kiss

Wind died down
Rain dwindles
Gently into a mist
As did we
Now forever gone

THUNDER

When we met
The thunder I felt
Was so powerful
So overwhelming
So loud
I must have appeared as a lamb

Getting to know you
Falling in love with you
Knowing you
Falling out of love with you
Lightning struck
Shedding my cloying wool
To be reborn
Emerging as a warrior

<u>THE JOKER</u>

Me and Thee

The world not to see

Hidden behind masks

Lurk many emotions

Too tender to see daylight

Shy becomes bold

The bold become shy

      And

The Joker becomes the Poet

Spilling truths so intense and tender

Leaving echoes that linger

<u>DREAM</u>

It was a strange dream

Flowers

And a note

"I love you"

Sending both to me

Telepathically

Leaving me puzzled

And hopeful

<u>SEASON</u>

We are only able to love

To the depths of our emotions

Some days, we are a bottomless fountain

Other days, an arid wasteland

We must come prepared

Some days are sunny and bright

Filled with laughter and gentle touches

Others are dark, wet and cold

Where nothing grows

And we grow scared

Days change

We change

Love has its own season

Changing with the wind

Sometimes caught

Sometimes not

<u>ECHOES</u>

Your name echoes
In my empty heart
The tears still fall
The void you created
A vacuous pit of particles
Flowing into a salty reservoir
Rusting any intrusion

GypsySong 2019

OLD FASHIONED

Old fashioned values
Put to the test of time
Some faded or obsolete
Strong yet crumbling into obsolesce
Evanescing to memory
As the world moves on
And the genteel remain
Strong and staid

TRIGGERS

We know not another's battle
Knowing would not mean understanding
We process thought and experiences
Differently
We can't fully comprehend another's
Triggers
And that is a blessing
Someone needs to be
There
To catch your fall
And dry your tears
Supplying the glue
To help you heal

<u>SMILE</u>

She shines through the darkest pain
And her lowest hour
So others may be comfortable
In their blindness
While her descent continues
Unnoticed by all

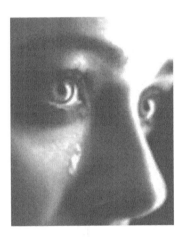

<u>WINTER CHILL</u>

The winter chill
Is reminiscent of your heart
Before you let me in
And the fire began

KISS MY TEARS

Make the tears stop
Quiet this loneliness
Wrap your arms around me
Like you plan to stay
Promise me the morning
Hours of rapt attention
Tell my heart what it needs to hear
Flowers to dilute this gloom
Sunshine to light my eyes
Reach my soul with tender smiles
Kiss my tears and my fears away
Make me feel safe
Make me feel loved

FIREFLIES AND MOONLIT SKIES

Turn out the lights

Let the summer steam settle in

Give inspiration to your imagination

Follow the break from darkness

Illuminated fireflies

Signaling for a mate

Teasing us with magic

PLUS ONE

I am tired of being alone
Being the plus one minus one
Putting on makeup that no one will see
Shaving legs that no one will feel
Yes, I cherish my independence
But I want to be able to decide when
I wear this cloak

FALLING TEARS

I held your hand
I dried your tears
I listened and let you know
You were not alone
You have grown since then
You now hold your tears in
As your heart breaks
But you won't let me in
Now my heart breaks
And I am alone
Funny how life
Changes us

FOUND: *UNICORN*

Why not

Just admit

You found

Your unicorn

And he

Wasn't strong

Enough

To survive

Your love?

<u>MISSED OPPORTUNITIES</u>

Things to say
Things to do
And it is all about you
Missed opportunities to speak
    My hearts soliloquy
    On star filled nights
    Atop mountain vistas
    Amid sandy dunes
    In full daylight
Today will be different
Today I will open up
Sharing my secrets
    My hopes
    My fears
Hoping you will share yours
And that you feel the same

<u>DUET</u>

I will follow you in the darkness

Letting you lead the way

Deeper into the night

Listening for crickets and frogs

As they lounge at water's edge

Calling for a mate

To sing a duet

And turn longing into love

VACUUM

A poet without words

No muse

No inspiration

Trapped between desire

And an empty vacuum

Begging for release

Needing air to breathe

Escape to survive

Love to sustain

Words to bloom

<u>LOST WORDS</u>

Poets who have lost their words
In a pain that is too deep
    Too dark
    Too painful
Can find solace in other artists work
Whether it be words or music or art
A connection is made
Raising the poet from
The drowning depths of despair
To where they are able
To breathe and bleed words
Once again

The Lone Wolf Series

Gypsy Mercer

LONE WOLF

His head turned and his eyes met mine
I felt their hypnotic effect
He was a lone wolf
That would never change
And I knew in that instant
I had no power against him
He could take
More than I knew how to give
And I would let him
I trembled as I smiled

The Lone Wolf Series

Gypsy Mercer

<u>HOWL</u>

Your head is down

Your ears are alert

Your eyes hiding black orbs

Behind lidded curtains

Waiting

Watching

You sense an intrusion

You know its source

Your muscles tense

Your head thrown back

As your loud

    Mournful

    Howl

Fills the air

Your wild is back

And won't be denied

The Lone Wolf Series

LEAVE

Leave!

I was here first

This is my world

My kingdom

My domain

I don't always play nicely with others

I know you mean me harm

But it works both ways

One of us

Needs to turn and walk away

But it will not be me

This is my home

Leave and live

Or prepare for death

This is not a game

It is life or loss

And I choose life

<u>SILENCE</u>

I enjoy silence

My thoughts tripping to destinations

Of my choosing

Compromise is not my game

I strike out alone

And enjoy the peace

That comes from

Being with myself

The Lone Wolf Series

RIPPLES

The gentle ripples of the water
Before the day dawns
Crickets winding down their mating calls
Fish kissing their oxygen bubbles
Calm before the days storm
I stand staring at my spirit image
Enjoying the fading peace
Today I hunt alone
Share my path with none
Experience sights and sounds
To feed my soul
Returning to my pack
Refreshed and sure

The Lone Wolf Series

<u>WEARY</u>

Today
I need you to take the lead
My trust in you is absolute
I observe your actions
Reactions
And I support them
Today I am tired
I want to just follow your lead
My head and heart are heavy
And weary
I am on automatic
Letting my soul repair itself
Force me out of
Complacency
If you need me
I wear my armor
And stroke my weapons
Always ready when you
Need me

Always at your side

Tomorrow

I will lead

Letting your

Mind and soul

Recharge

It is the basis

Of Two Alpha' s

Commitment

And connection

Severed only through death

The Lone Wolf Series

<u>**HABITAT**</u>

I need no one

I walk alone

Separate myself from the pack

Discover new things

    About myself

    About my habitat

Smell fresh scents

Not diluted

By secretions of those

Who walked before me

I test my reflexes

With the hunt

Enjoy my rewards

Then retreat

Into the night

And begin anew

The Lone Wolf Series

<u>THOUGHTS</u>

I am by his side
Or in his thoughts
Always

The Lone Wolf Series

Gypsy Mercer

A WOLF

A wolf is not always a wolf

Nor is it always an animal

Or beast

Sometimes it appears

As a dream

Our imagination will not release

Whose spirit hunts

And haunts us

Sometimes it is a memory

At the edge of capture

Sometimes it is a hunger

We are unable to quench

Sometimes it is our spirit guide

Teaching us lessons

While guarding our soul

Sometimes it is our soul

Hoping for peace

And release

The Lone Wolf Series

UNITED

His howl pierces the night

My soulful response follows

We crash through time

To find each other

No soul

No object

Will keep us apart

Your scent fills my nostrils with yearning

Your blood pumps harder

Your touch draws me in

United once again

The Lone Wolf Series

Gypsy Mercer

<u>WHIPPOORWILL</u>

The evening just taking hold

The moon lighting the sky

Gentle breezes after a scorching day

Serenity

Smiling

Lighthearted

The birds calling

Singing

Trilling

The whippoorwill beckoning

Promising

Love

Pure love

True love

Agape

And I said a silent prayer

Of thanks

<u>FORK IN THE ROAD</u>

The air is chilled

My coat is damp

The air so clean

And I am safe

Wondering if you are too

The road forked

Causing our paths to dissect

Feeling incomplete

I cry into the night

Needing to connect

Your answering call

Reassures me

Tomorrow we travel back

And again hunt as one

The Lone Wolf Series

<u>BATTLE WORN</u>

Battle worn and weary

Circling the camp

Assessing damages

Confident strides

Disguising my pain

Sentries posted

Allowing us

To rest and recharge

Tomorrow is a new day

And we will attack

With sovereignty

Taking

What is rightfully ours

Annihilating our enemies

Giving warning

To other pretenders

The Lone Wolf Series

<u>UNINHIBITED</u>

You woke the beast in me

The one with pure

Uninhibited

Reactions

No longer in control

Responding to your Alpha

Your needs

Satisfying mine

In the process

Begging for more

The Lone Wolf Series

<u>FIGHT</u>

Don't mistake my patience
For weakness
I see and feel all things
When I am ready
I will fight for you
Or not
My choice

The Lone Wolf Series

SEA OF PEOPLE

Glancing around the sea of people

I found your eyes

Staring back at me

Not lewd nor suggestive

They simple absorbed me

You did not look away

And I could not

Be it seconds or minutes

I do not know

But a smile slowly emerged

From your full lips

Mirroring mine

Your eyes shone brighter

Some call it a twinkle

You then walked toward me

With sure footed grace

Erasing all in your path

I was frozen in time

Waiting for my Alpha

To make a home

In my soul

The Lone Wolf Series

PRIMED

Your magnificence is unparalleled
Your stance
    So proud
    So regal
Unconcerned with trivia
You have fought enough battles
That defeat is no longer entertained
The air you breathe is fresh
Scented by aspen
Adrenaline
Cruising through your veins
Filling you with
Strength
Determination
Primed for the fight

The Lone Wolf Series

<u>MY ALPHA</u>

My dear Alpha
You have misjudged me
You saw me as your infatuated lamb
Eager for your attention
With no mind of my own.
Your underestimation
Allowed me to get beneath your skin
Cradling your heart
Now there are two of us
Drowning in this passionate
Cataclysmic collision

The Lone Wolf Series

<u>I WALK ALONE</u>

I walk alone

By choice

Unhindered

By opinions

Or compromise

Seeking my own pleasure

Satisfying my primal need

To digest first

Anything that appeals to me

My senses

My imagination

Until I am satiated

And move on

The Lone Wolf Series

BEAST

Arrows deflect off my armor
Bullets ricochet
Once your call was my command
Now your voice no longer soothes me
Nor lures me into your trap
I learned the hard way
That honey attracts any manner of beast
And that I was your beast

The Lone Wolf Series

<u>THE HUNT</u>

Sitting in our private place

Listening for sounds

Distinguishing normal

From new

Or missing

Cataloguing

Anticipating

Preparing

For the hunt

The hunt that confirms my dominance

And crowns me Alpha

The Lone Wolf Series

<u>VIOLENCE</u>

Violence will follow

Should you deign

To trespass

With intentions toward my Alpha

Be you friend or enemy

Battle will be immediate

And vicious

As will your death

The Lone Wolf Series

<u>DOMINANCE</u>

No need for arrogance

Nor aggression

We know that I am

Your Alpha

The oldest

The wisest

The strongest

My love and passion

Run deep

I will guide you

And protect you

Because you are

My entire world

The Lone Wolf Series

<u>BREATHE</u>

My strength is for myself
    My pack
    My family
    For my Alpha
I do not accept trespass
    From strangers
    From Betas
I fight battles to win
I do not accept defeat
I will fight until
Death
Using my last breathe
To protect those I love
As the gods
Bring me home
Howling
For Mother Moon

The Lone Wolf Series

HEART BEAT

At times

We travel different paths

It does not mean we are separate

As our psyche is still connected

I see your face

I sense your presence

I feel your love

Lone Wolf you may be

But our hearts beat as one

And we are never alone

The Lone Wolf Series

<u>BOUND</u>

I walk among wolves

They accept me as I am

No fear

Just respect

This is my pack

I fought and I won

Now I lead and they follow

They honor the Alpha in me

My Alpha walks toward me

My mate

Bound for life

I no longer prowl alone

The Lone Wolf Series

FERAL

Your feral nature

Commands my attention

You are inside my head

You hear my thoughts

You answer my call

Yet you invite me into your heart

Knowing

I will fiercely protect you

With my last breath

As you will for me

The Lone Wolf Series

NO HESITATION

I walk beside you

Shoulder to shoulder

Matching your gait

You scan right

I take left

No hesitation

Just intuition

We have followed this trail before

Separate yet together

We hunt as one

No competition

Just trust and loyalty

My Alpha and me

The Lone Wolf Series

RETURN

You left before dawn

Some journeys are alone

This is one

My heart is with you

My mind is comforting you on every step

Think of me in the shadows

Believing in you

Loving you

I would move mountains

Just to ease your journey

And to see happiness in your eyes

And relief in your heart

Lone Wolf you may be

But my heart beats in yours

Wherever you may travel

Awaiting your safe return

The Lone Wolf Series

FADING

Your step is sure
But slower than once
Your keen sight
Catalogs the terrain
The experiences of previous battles
Is at your beck and call
Calculations of gain or loss
Weigh heavily in your thoughts
Understanding strategy is different
From implementing it
Support for your decisions
Is absolute
But you know it is positioning
For you are fading
Into the past
Making room for the new Alpha

The Lone Wolf Series

<u>WARMTH</u>

My eyes are closed
Feeling the warmth of the sun
Acknowledging its healing powers
After a brutal winter
The electrical charge in the air
Sparking with intensity
The peace that assails my body
The surrender to bliss
As my Alpha stands guard
Insuring our safety

The Lone Wolf Series

<u>PATIENT</u>

I am patient

I will wait

Until you are most vulnerable

I will attack

Enjoy destroying you

As you have done

To those

I swore to protect and love

And I will not be patient

Nor kind

Your defeat

Is my only redemption

The Lone Wolf Series

<u>UNISON</u>

A peace

A calmness

So serene that our souls

Purr in unison

The ecstasy rises

Tickling our throats

Begging for release

Without conscious thought

Softly

Hauntingly

Escaping

Our howl claims the night

The Lone Wolf Series

ENEMY

Your enemies are my enemies

Never doubt me

Trust me

For a time I will not walk beside you

My heart and my loyalty remain with you

But in war

Know your foe

Study your prey

Plan your attack

Follow through

Don't step back

Walk away with the crown

Then return home

The Lone Wolf Series

<u>RAIN</u>

The rain
    Mutes scents
    Dilutes tracks
    Distorts sounds
But I am patient
Knowing
The Hunt will begin soon

The Lone Wolf Series

FEED THE WOLF

We travel as one
Registering all in our sight
Cataloging smells and sounds
Indigenous to the region
Startled responses
To our presence
Is normal
And noted
The exodus is expected
And frenzied

The Lone Wolf Series

Gypsy Mercer

Just because

~ GypsySong

Gypsy Mercer

<u>MASQUERADE</u>

I am who I need to be in the moment. My whole life has been about sorting, categorizing and placing those thoughts, those people, in cages or boxes. When my ego or my heart or my soul has a need, I go to that shelf and select what I need, feeding my addiction, selecting that which fills me, heals me. Needs may vary, answers can change. We are able to stop time in our head and daydream, but life moves on. When you find that a certain persona no longer serves you, you either abandon it or change it.

My masks come in many shades and hues.

165

<u>TWO HALVES</u>

Please don't make me choose
Loving you both
Fills my universe
Two halves
    Separate and complete
    Different yet the same
Together you answer my needs
I always give you 100 percent
I always give him 100 percent
Just not at the same time
I am here when you want me
Or need me
Not everyone is two dimensional
Some of us hunger for more
Than one can provide
And seek to fill the voids

It does not lessen you

Because you become

An intricate part

Of my hearts puzzle

Chaos ensues when pieces

Are messing

The picture becomes

Distorted

And cannot be made whole

SOMEONE TO LOVE

Searching for someone to love
And I found it within
Then turned my heart
Toward the light
And found yet another
Willing heart
To share the flight

SKELETONS

I can't help you

You are holding onto a dream

Once technicolor

Now faded to black and white

More reminiscent of ghosts

Or nightmares dancing

With the skeleton of your dreams

It doesn't get better

Gather all that has value to you

Set fire to the rest

From the ashes you shall rise

Your strength increasing

With each breath

Your mind freeing itself

From the shackles

That held you in check

Free to love

Free to live

169

<u>**LETTERS**</u>

Found letters I had written you
So many years ago
I never intended to send them
Just wanted to purge my thoughts
Without recourse
So used ink instead of voice
I was amazed that
I remembered you
   So much kinder
   So much more loving
Years dull the edge
Rounding corners
On the sharp edges
My anger toward you
Became perceived inadequacies in me
How could I love someone
As callous and cold as you?
 Did our passion override reality?

Why did it take so long to see you
Remember you
Without the halo I drew on
Your ghost?
How could you say that
You loved me
When it was only the pieces
Of your choosing?
I loved you more than life itself
More than the air I breathed
But you made me choose
And I did
The scars from loving you
Remain today
Tainting my heart

<u>ART</u>

A poet's art

Is their heart

Original

Passionate

Raw

Pure

Sometimes filled with darkness

Sometimes light

Never a shadow

To their lover's delight

<u>YOUTH</u>

I beg to differ. This saddens me. Antiques have stood the test of time. Experience teaches us patience. Originals are a work of art. Fine wine develops superbly with the years. The Classics are revered. Poetry had rhyme.

Youth is youth...and it fades
And cannot be resurrected
Much to our sorrow
Much to our delight

Gypsy Mercer

LOVE LIKE A POET

Let me love like a poet
Without boundaries
Without permission
Without regret
Without restraint

Let my words speak to his heart
In endless languages
With delicate nuances clear to the two of us
With deep stirrings
With sacred truths
And titanic promises

Let me be loved by a Poet
Unafraid to express his yearnings
Verbose in his descriptions
Tender in his touch
Furious in his passion

Let me hear his words float

Throughout my body

Opening veins once damaged

Now fragile

Massaging away doubt

Creating our personal fortress

So we may speak beyond words

And love without fear.

<u>TIRED</u>

Do you get tired of doing the right thing
    Always picking up pieces
    Carrying the burdensome load
    Accepting the short end of the stick
    Saying "yes" when you mean "no"
Do you think God is keeping score
Balancing the rights
    Against so many wrongs
Are you paying ahead
    Hoping for one last big hoorah
Does the payment of a smile
    Or a thank you
No longer seem enough
I think I am tired and
Just maybe
I want to drop my load

Maybe I want someone to carry me

While I fill my cup

With love and ----

Just enough

To do the right thing

BUTTERFLY KISSES

Dear Future Perfect Me,

I hope you remember when Fairy Tales and
Ferris wheels taught you to believe
    ...we could touch the sky
    ...when butterfly kisses turned to
      frog princes
    ...when Christmas trumped every other
      day of the year
    ...and wishes were promises that were
      never broken
    ...when a hug was a hug
    ...and a kiss healed everything

Remember kinder days and infuse them
into your difficult days. Let that magic of
your youth guide you and feed you, and
continue to plant flowers that grow.

<u>PUZZLE</u>

Square edges are easy to work with

Empty a puzzle box

Tightly lock the perimeter

It is the other pieces that cause

The difficulty

Rounded corners

Sharp points

Ocean inlets in a sea of colors

Ambiguous angles

Selecting pieces that might fit

Seems endless

Twisting, turning

Finally the last piece snaps in place

The euphoria

The sense of completion

The psychic satisfaction

That rights your world

And makes your heart smile

<u>YOU WOULD NOT UNDERSTAND</u>

If I left you
    You would know
But may not understand
If I stay
    You know that I will try
We hurt each other without intent
That is what scares me the most
How can two people so in love
Regularly cause so much pain?
Is there a settling factor
    That will end this dance?
Can we fast forward this pain
    And give each other one last chance?
Can we wake tomorrow
    And end this show?
 Can we kiss the wounds
    And have them disappear?
Can faith be rebuilt?

Our love is deep
    And so are we
Can we commit without fear?
Pledging our hearts
    And our dreams
To starlit nights
Chasing fireflies
Inhaling the night air
Touching the dew
While being serenaded
    By lonesome creatures
      Seeking their mate
Preserving the magic
  In our hearts?
And if I left
It was because
I kept breaking
    My heart
While breaking yours
And it could not go on

<u>GYPSY BLOOD</u>

I was a young girl

Learning to please

Learning to tease

I have grown up since then

I no longer sit at your feet

Adoring as a new puppy

I have claws

And Gypsy blood

That boils with passion

Eyes that flash danger

Or at any lie

I move with grace and surety

Crawling under your skin

Assaulting your senses

Claiming your soul

Walk or run

To or from

Perhaps you should find a kitten

That doesn't leave marks

Index

Title	Page

**The Lone Wolf Series

<u>*Who is Gypsy Mercer?*</u>

She is a girl that turned into a woman who read poetry and believed in Knights and magic.

Gypsy began writing in college when she found that her thoughts and written prose were so much more powerful than speaking her truth.

Life and reality forced a hiatus while she raised a family and made her way into the professional world. All along, she believed that her real world was in opposition to the needs of her heart and her soul. No longer constrained, she picked up her pen freeing both.

This is the result of her escape from captivity.

Follow Gypsy Mercer
www.GypsyMercer.com
Facebook: GypsySong
Instagram: @MercerGypsy

Gypsy Mercer

Made in United States
Orlando, FL
03 November 2022

24177555R00104